D1462196

"The architecture of peace
relies on the entire world."
Paul Éluard and Pablo Picasso, *The Face of Peace*, 1951.


*For Ireneo and his peace-bearing name.*
G. E.


*For Tom.*
Z.

© for the French edition: L´Élan vert, Saint-Pierre-des-Corps, 2017
Title of the original edition: *Les Deux Colombes*
© for the English edition: Prestel Verlag, Munich • London • New York, 2017
A member of Verlagsgruppe Random House GmbH
Neumarkter Strasse 28 · 81673 Munich
© for the work by Pablo Picasso: Succession Picasso, 2017
© Photo: Parisienne de photographie / Pablo Picasso / Musée d'Art moderne

Prestel Publishing Ltd.
14-17 Wells Street
London W1T 3PD

Prestel Publishing
900 Broadway, Suite 603
New York, NY 10003

In respect to links in the book, the Publisher expressly notes that no illegal content was
discernible on the linked sites at the time the links were created. The Publisher has no
influence at all over the current and future design, content or authorship of the linked
sites. For this reason the Publisher expressly disassociates itself from all content on
linked sites that has been altered since the link was created and assumes no liability for
such content.

Library of Congress Control Number: 2017938211
A CIP catalogue record for this book is available from the British Library.

Translated from the French by Agathe Joly
Copy-editing: Brad Finger
Project management: Melanie Schöni
Production management and typesetting: Corinna Pickart
Printing and binding: TBB, a.s. Banská Bystrica
Paper: Condat matt Périgord

MIX
From responsible
sources
FSC® C022120

Verlagsgruppe Random House FSC® N001967

Printed in Slovakia

ISBN 978-3-7913-7330-0
www.prestel.com

# The Two Doves

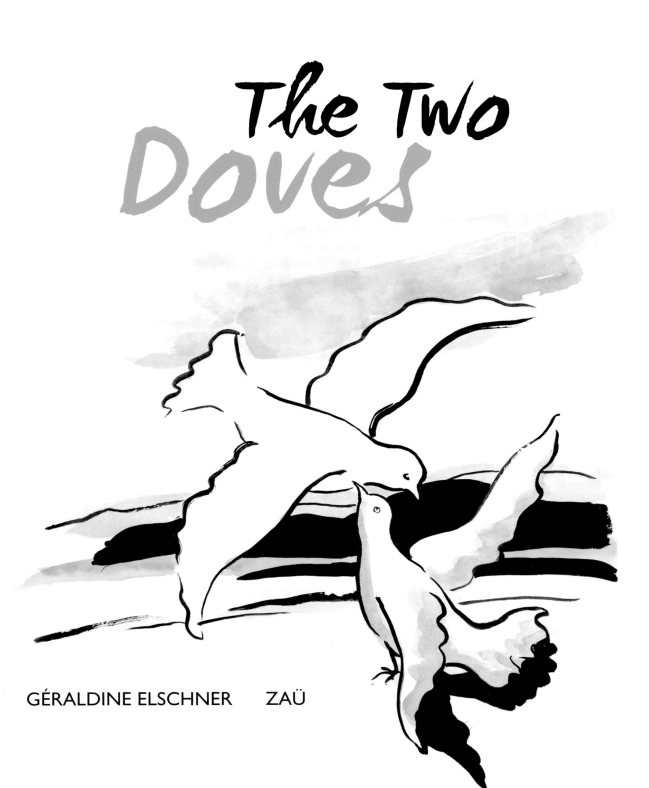

GÉRALDINE ELSCHNER     ZAÜ

PRESTEL

MUNICH · LONDON · NEW YORK

For how long had it been flying so swiftly,
a small dot in the great big sky?
Under its feet, as far as it could see, the sea was shining
like a mirror that had swallowed everything.

When, at last, its round and sharp eye caught a glimpse
of an island on the horizon,
it felt invigorated by a new strength. Water! Grain!
It would soon be able to feed and rest.
Instantly, the dove headed to the rocks.

But this moment of joy was short-lived. The land there was firm but
very hard, and so dry that nothing could grow on it. All around there
were only dried out fields, rock plants, deserted barns. At the center
of the island stood a strange mountain made of unusual
objects piled on top of one another.

On what planet had it landed?
A lifeless planet without grass or water,
covered in garbage, which suffocated the ground ...
Disappointed, the dove resumed its flight.

The second island seemed smaller but beautiful,
surrounded by multicolored flags flapping in the wind.
They led to an immense big top: a circus!
The dove flew up to it. The ring was empty ...
On a chair there was only a forgotten guitar
placed atop a Harlequin's costume.
But where were the performers? The clown with the red nose?
The tightrope walker? The acrobats?

Not far from there was a third island, also deserted.
Of the towns and villages that once stood there,
only ruins remained amidst the darkened trunks of trees.
The people from the countryside had flown.
Everything had been destroyed.

Exhausted, the dove took shelter for the night
at the foot of a statue. It was then that it saw, ...

huddled against a stone, a dove with a grey and blue head
lying in the dust. Its chest bore a red stain,
marked with a long black line.
It was barely breathing.
White as snow, the traveling dove lay
against it to bring it warmth. In the rubble
it found a few scraps of bread that it slipped, piece by piece,
into the hungry beak. It also collected
some water, drop by drop, into a lace parasol.

In the early morning the blue dove raised its head.
Its beautiful purple round eye seemed to say:
"I'm wounded but alive! Thanks to you, my friend, thank you!"

A few days later, under a setting sun,
they took to the sky, the one leading the other.
Out there a great ark marked the horizon,
and underneath it a fine green line emerged.
Was this a forest?

The coast followed the curve of the sea,
where it was met by a river.
Flying against the current,
the dove saw a house
surrounded by a large garden.
Under an old olive tree,
a man was painting on an easel
with children playing around him.

"Look!," cried out Olivia
as she caught sight of the two birds.
The two friends raised their heads,
but at that very moment
the exhausted blue dove fell
to their feet. The little girl
took it in her arms.

"It's wounded," said Olivia. "We must heal it."
"I'll take care of it!," said one of the boys.
"No, me!," answered the youngest.
"I will take care of it," said the eldest of the group.
As if to reconcile them, the white dove
flew from one to the other, tracing a small circle
above their heads.
"Nobody move! Hand me my brushes!,"
 said Picasso.

And Pablo drew and drew,
and the children began to calm down and paint beside him.
Their drawings were soon hanging on the washing line.
But suddenly ...

a great burst of wind shook up the garden, and before the small group had time
to react, the paper birds flew out from their makeshift perch.
In the crazy wind they began to whirl faster and faster, higher and higher.

Delighted, the children gathered around Pablo
to watch them go up and up.
"How far will they go?," asked Olivia.
"They'll go to countries all around the world," answered Pablo, dreamily.

As the paper birds were about to disappear amidst the clouds, the white dove spread its wings. It was time to leave. There, on the other side of the earth, on the other side of time, other children were waiting. With a branch of olive tree in its beak, the timeless wanderer swiftly renewed its endless journey, a small white dot in the great big sky. The blue dove huddled in Olivia's arms. Here it could live in peace.

# Pablo Picasso
## (1881-1973)

# The Dove of Peace

Pastel
23 x 31 cm
circa 1950
Paris,
Musée d'Art Moderne de la Ville de Paris

## Picasso's name is famous, but *what is he known for?*

Born 1881 in Málaga in southern Spain, he was the son of a painter. Close to great artists, poets and painters, he invented Cubism with his painter friend Georges Braque. And what was Cubism? It was a revolution in painting that refused to imitate reality. Instead, it depicted objects, figures and faces as geometric shapes.

Picasso explored until his death (in 1973) all forms of art: painting, sculpture, ceramics, metalworking, linocut prints. Nothing escaped his creative genius.
Pablo's works are displayed all around the world. In Paris, a museum is dedicated entirely to him: the Picasso Museum.

## Is this the first time that Picasso worked *for peace?*

No. In 1937, during the Spanish Civil War, the small Basque town of Guernica in northern Spain was bombarded. The outcome: 1,654 deaths. The whole world grieved for Guernica and Picasso made a painting for the Universal Exhibition in Paris. Entitled *Guernica*, it's a large black and white canvas that speaks of mourning. Its expressive strength makes it an international icon for peace, the power of which remains alive today.

## Why did Picasso draw *this dove?*

In 1949, after the horrors of World War II had ended, writers, artists and other thinkers gathered together to work for peace. They called their meeting the World Congress of Partisans for Peace. When choosing a picture to represent the Congress, writer Louis Aragon selected a lithograph print by Picasso. This print, however, showed a pigeon and not a dove! For the second Congress, which took place in Sheffield, England in 1950, Picasso engraved a white dove in full flight. Pablo's image soon became a worldwide symbol for peace.

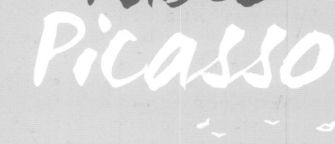

# Pablo Picasso

## Did Picasso paint *other doves?*

Pigeons and doves are common in Picasso's work, symbols that were charged with emotion since his childhood. Like his artist friend Henri Matisse, Picasso owned pigeons; and when he opened their cage, which he often did, they would perch themselves on his head or shoulders. Picasso learned to study and depict birds from his father, Ruiz. He re-created them with various techniques: drawing, sculpting, and painting. According to legend, when Picasso was 13 years old, his father asked him to draw the feet of a dead pigeon. Pablo's drawing was so lifelike, Ruiz declared that his son had already become a greater artist than he was!
Picasso's work includes a lot of other pigeons and doves: *Child with a Dove* painted in 1901, where a small child in a long white robe holds a white dove against his chest; *The Pigeon with Green Peas* (1911); *Still Life with Pigeon* (1919); and the many many doves of peace, with or without an olive branch, flowers or angelic faces of women. In 1949, Picasso even named his second daughter Paloma, a name that means dove in Spanish.

# WHERE on EARTH?

# SOUTH AMERICA

By Shalini Vallepur

Designed by Brandon Mattless

S00000910267

## Photo Credits

All images are courtesy of Shutterstock.com, unless otherwise specified. With thanks to Getty Images, Thinkstock Photo and iStockphoto. Front Cover - LineTale, Maquiladora, Shanvood, Sky and glass, StockSmartStart, Seita, Ricky Edwards, Tartila, Shtonado, GoodStudio. Recurring Images – Apostrophe, Attitude, Kharchenko Ruslan, Miro Novak, winnond, Daria Yakovleva, Yaska, Maquiladora, Amanita Silvicora, Irina Danyliuk, Annasunny24. 4–5 – Benn Beckman, Annasunny24. 6–7 – Alan Falcony, Cezary Wojtkowski, Ksenia Ragozina, Peter Hermes Furian. 8–9 – Rawpixel.com. 10–11 – D'July, streetflash. 12–13 – danceyourlife, Jess Kraf, streetflash, The Hornbills Studio, Toniflap. 14–15 – Janossy Gergely, Pavel Svoboda Photography. 16–17 – boreala, f11photo, rodrigo gavini. 18–19 – MarySan, buteo, Dr Morley Read, guentermanaus. 20–21 – Ekaterina Pokrovsky, Filip Bjorkman, Michele Rinaldil, sunsinger. 22–23 – Food Via Lenses, ilkayalptekin, Louno Morose, MIMOgo, Natykach Nataliia, nehophoto, Peruphotart, Tomacco.

Words that look like **this** can be found in the glossary on page 24.

DUDLEY LIBRARIES

| DUDLEY LIBRARIES | |
| --- | --- |
| S00000910267 | |
| Askews & Holts | 06-Jan-2022 |
| C918 | £7.99 |
| 2SLS | |

Written by:
Shalini Vallepur

## BookLife PUBLISHING

©2021
BookLife Publishing Ltd.
King's Lynn
Norfolk PE30 4LS

ISBN: 978-1-83927-202-8

Edited by:
William Anthony

Designed by:
Brandon Mattless

All rights reserved.
Printed in Malaysia.

A catalogue record for this book is available from the British Library.

All facts, statistics, web addresses and URLs in this book were verified as valid and accurate at time of writing. No responsibility for any changes to external websites or references can be accepted by either the author or publisher.